# A STARLET'S
# SHADOW

Book design by Sarah Taplin
Cover illustration by Maggie Ivy
Interior illustrations by Clonefront Entertainment (Beehive Illustration)

Published in the United States by Jolly Fish Press, an imprint of North Star Editions, Inc.

First Edition
First Printing, 2019

This is a work of fiction. Names, characters, places, and incidents are either the product of the author's imagination or are used fictitiously, and any resemblance to actual persons living or dead, business establishments, events, or locales is entirely coincidental.

**Library of Congress Cataloging-in-Publication Data**
Names: Troupe, Thomas Kingsley, author.
Title: A starlet's shadow / by Thomas Kingsley Troupe.
Description: First edition. | Mendota Heights, MN : Jolly Fish Press, [2020] |
    Summary: When sisters Isabella and Marta Rodriguez visit Aunt Violeta in
    California, it is up to Isabella to figure out what the ghost of Hollywood
    Hills wants.
Identifiers: LCCN 2018060109 (print) | LCCN 2019004294 (ebook) | ISBN
    9781631633614 (ebook) | ISBN 9781631633607 (pbk.) | ISBN 9781631633591
    (hardcover)
Subjects: | CYAC: Ghosts—Fiction. | Actors and actresses—Fiction. |
    Sisters—Fiction. | Aunts—Fiction. | Hollywood (Los Angeles,
    Calif.)—Fiction. | Chilean Americans—Fiction. | LCGFT: Ghost stories. |
    Fiction.
Classification: LCC PZ7.T7538 (ebook) | LCC PZ7.T7538 Ss 2019 (print) | DDC
    [Fic]—dc23
LC record available at https://lccn.loc.gov/2018060109

Jolly Fish Press
North Star Editions, Inc.
2297 Waters Drive
Mendota Heights, MN 55120
www.jollyfishpress.com

Printed in the United States of America

HAUNTED STATES
of
AMERICA

# A STARLET'S

# SHADOW

## THOMAS KINGSLEY TROUPE

JOLLY
FiSH
PRESS
Mendota Heights, Minnesota

# CHAPTER 1

# VACATION

*It's like a whole different world,* Isabella Rodriguez realized.

She watched the endless line of shops they passed on Hollywood Boulevard from the backseat of her aunt's car. She spotted the salmon-colored granite stars lining the sidewalk with gold borders around them and the gold names of famous people stamped in the middle. She smiled at the palm trees planted along the sidewalks. People were stopping along the crowded sidewalks in front of landmarks along the way to take photos and selfies. She lost count of how many tattoo parlors she saw.

It was the first time she and her older sister, Marta, had visited Aunt Violeta at her home on the West Coast. Just from the sunshine alone, Isa could see why the Golden State was California's nickname.

Everything seemed busy and crowded and hectic in Los Angeles—even more so in Hollywood, which Aunt

Violeta was quick to point out "isn't actually a city," but a neighborhood in LA.

Isa held up her camera, rolled down the window, and took a picture of a man dressed as a superhero leaning against a streetlight. He'd pulled up his webbed red mask a bit to expose his mouth so he could eat a donut.

*You just don't see that kind of thing in Des Moines,* Isa thought. She was definitely going to post that one online. *Don't worry, super guy. Your identity is safe with me.*

"Are you girls hungry for lunch?" Aunt Violeta asked from the driver's seat.

"Yeah, I could eat my arm," Marta said.

"Oh, don't do that," Aunt Violeta replied, sounding a bit worried. "There are plenty of restaurants out here."

Isa laughed. The way her aunt responded made it seem like she thought Marta was seriously considering turning her arm into a meal. She must not have picked up on Marta's sarcasm, or maybe she just didn't find it funny.

"I'm a little hungry too," Isa replied. They hadn't eaten much at the theme park for fear of getting sick on the rides. But after driving more than an hour back from Anaheim, she was ready to eat too. Probably not her arm though.

"There's a good place up ahead," Aunt Violeta said. "It's been around forever. It'll be a good first dinner for you in Hollyweird."

*Hollyweird?* Isa thought.

She looked out the window and saw a woman with spiky purple hair, black makeup around her eyes, and at least fifty piercings in her nose. A live parrot was sitting on her shoulder.

Isa knew what her aunt meant.

———

When Isa stepped into Frank & Marty's Grill, it felt like she'd used a time machine to rocket sixty years into the past. The neon signs out front had announced it was the oldest restaurant in Hollywood, having opened its doors in 1919.

She could see why.

The inside of the restaurant was mostly dark, with light sconces on the walls above the booths. There were white linen tablecloths on the tables, and fancy dim light fixtures were suspended from the ornate ceiling.

"Whoa," Marta said. "This place is old."

"And fancy," Isa added. She raised her camera and took a quick picture.

There was a man with a mustache and a smile

waiting at the host booth for them. He was dressed in a sharp black tuxedo and looked like he'd walked off the set from the kind of movies her grandma liked to watch.

Isa felt severely underdressed in her shorts and T-shirt.

"Aunt Violeta," Isa said. "You sure we belong here?"

Aunt Violeta waved her niece away like she was being ridiculous.

"Don't be silly," she replied. "*They* have to dress fancy. We don't!"

The host took them through the restaurant to a small table in the back corner. They passed waiters in bright-red suitcoats and people enjoying their meals and quiet conversation. Isa could say hands down it was the fanciest place she'd ever been to.

"They're putting us in the back because we look like tourists," Marta whispered. "That's so we don't make the place look bad."

Isa shrugged. *"Okay."*

The three of them took their seat at the table and smiled at one another. Isa found she was almost afraid to touch anything for fear of messing it up.

"Isn't this great?" Aunt Violeta squealed and clapped

her hands lightly to try and contain her excitement. "A whole week with my two favorite nieces!"

Isa raised her eyebrows. She wondered what her cousins Luz and Renata would think if they heard their aunt say that. Considering they still lived in Chile, she guessed it didn't make much difference.

*And they're probably her favorite nieces when she goes down to visit them,* Isa thought.

"Don't turn your head, but I think that's the guy from the *Werewolf Journals* show," Marta said.

Aunt Violeta turned, making it completely obvious that she was stargazing.

"That guy?" their aunt asked.

Marta looked like she might melt in her seat just so she could dribble and hide under the table in embarrassment.

"Oh, Martalina," Aunt Violeta said. "He can't hear me."

"Really? I can't believe real actors and famous people eat here!" Isa exclaimed.

"I guess I hadn't noticed," Aunt Violeta replied.

She glanced briefly over her shoulder. Sitting at a nearby table was a man in his early twenties with slicked blond hair and teeth that looked impossibly clean. He was talking to a woman who wore her dark hair wrapped up into a bun on top of her head.

*It's him!* Isa had never seen a famous person in real life before. Two tables over, a real celebrity was eating some sort of pasta.

After calming down, the three of them ordered their food and something to drink. Isa thought everything on the menu was kind of expensive and pointed it out to her aunt. Aunt Violeta just shook her head and told her to order whatever she wanted.

"You only live once, Isabella," her aunt said. "And I don't see you often enough."

It was true. Ever since Aunt Violeta had moved from Des Moines, Iowa, to Los Angeles a few years ago, the best they could do was talk to each other from time to time through video chat. Having never visited their aunt on the West Coast, both Isa and Marta had jumped at the chance to go. This was the first time Isa and Marta had gotten to stay with Aunt Violeta, and it was for a whole week while their parents were on a business trip.

Compared to the flat farmland and small city they were used to back home, Los Angeles was a bit overwhelming. It was big, had incredible scenery– including the ocean—and traffic.

Lots and lots of traffic.

To kick off their trip, their aunt had taken them directly to the enormous theme park, right from the airport.

"Star treatment," Aunt Violeta had said. "We're going to pack in as much fun as possible!"

As they waited now for their food, they all looked around the restaurant for more famous faces. There was a guy who looked like he played the dad on *Our Apartment*, but it was hard to tell in the dim room.

Isa realized why they probably kept the lights low: It prevented regular people from spotting the rich and famous.

"I wish I was on TV," Marta said as the waiter arrived with their meals.

He set a French-dip sandwich in front of her and a grilled cheese in front of Isa. There were a few other things she wouldn't have minded having, but she felt bad that her aunt had already spent so much on them.

"I don't know," Isa said, thinking it over. "I'm not sure I'd like it."

"It's because you're shy," Marta said. "You don't like all the attention."

"Yeah, I suppose," Isa replied. "Maybe if I could try

being famous for a week. If I didn't like it, I want to be able to quit and go back to my regular life."

"Being famous?" Aunt Violeta asked, then shuddered as if the thought disgusted her. "No thanks. Too many people bugging you, following you around, staring at you at restaurants. I'd rather not bother with all of that. If you have friends, good health, and family, who needs fame?"

"That's true," Isa said, nodding. Marta shrugged.

With that, Aunt Violeta raised her glass. The Rodriguez sisters followed suit, tapping their soft drinks against their aunt's mineral water.

"Cheers, girls," Aunt Violeta said. "To being rich in family."

Isa smiled. She realized just then how much she'd missed her aunt.

———

It was a short drive from Frank & Marty's Grill to Aunt Violeta's house. All along the way, Isa saw fascinating houses, interesting people, and what looked like mountains. There were houses on stilts along the side and winding roads that would've been terrible to drive in the winter.

Something the people of California never had to worry about.

"What's the name of that big mountain?" Isa asked.

"You know, I thought you were adorable when you were born, Isabella," Aunt Violeta said, smiling at her through the rear-view mirror. "But fourteen years later, I think you might be even cuter."

*What did I say?* Isa wondered.

"That's Mount Lee," her aunt said. "Part of the Santa Monica Mountains. But no one really calls it that around here."

"Why not?" Marta asked. She leaned forward in the front seat to peer up at the slopes, peppered here and there with greenery.

"Because they're more widely known as the Hollywood Hills," Aunt Violeta replied.

Just then, as if she'd planned it, she turned, and their view of Mount Lee changed. There, standing tall over the houses below, were the nine letters that were, to some, considered more impressive than Mount Rushmore or the pyramids of Egypt: HOLLYWOOD.

"You live near the Hollywood sign?!" Isa cried, straining against her seatbelt to get a better view from the backseat.

"I do," Aunt Violeta replied. "My little place has a pretty good view of it. Paid dearly for it too, I'm afraid."

Their aunt turned left, giving Isa a much better view of the letters for a moment. The letters were bright, almost like they were glowing. As Isa raised up her phone to take a picture, trees and houses from the neighborhood blocked her view.

"I missed it," Isa said.

"Like I said," Aunt Violeta repeated, "you'll like the view from my house."

"Or, you know," Marta said, "you could try enjoying the sights with your own eyes, instead of taking a picture every two seconds."

Isa shook her head. At seventeen, Marta acted like she knew everything and thought she was the third parent, trying to boss Isa around. Isa found that the best solution was to ignore her, but sometimes, it wasn't easy.

*I'm going to have a ton of pictures to remember this place*, Isa thought. *Because who knows when we'll have the chance to come back?*

After another minute of driving, seeing just glimpses of the sign through trees and between houses, they finally arrived at Aunt Violeta's house.

The "little place" was anything but. The house was a

light-tan color, and there were pavers instead of grass. It wasn't a gigantic home, but it had a fancy archway over the brick driveway. Two palm trees grew up from the front yard, shading the house a little bit from the hot July sun.

"Wow!" Isa exclaimed. "This is a nice place!"

Isa knew that her aunt and uncle had always been pretty well-off, even when they had lived in Iowa. After Uncle Victor passed away a few years ago, her mom had said Aunt Violeta would still be comfortable financially living on her own.

"I think you'll like the backyard even more," Aunt Violeta said as she pulled into the driveway and parked the car.

The three of them left the suitcases behind, and the girls followed their aunt through a gateway. The back of the house was a large balcony held up above a valley in the hills with stilts. There was a nice seating area underneath an awning to provide shade. Further out was a swimming pool.

"Over here, over here," Aunt Violeta said, waving them over to the railing.

Isa and Marta walked over, both of their mouths hanging open in fascination.

As Isa got close, she saw her aunt hadn't been lying: The view of the Hollywood sign was incredible. It was off in the distance but seemed to somehow tower over them and the rest of Hollywood as if it were standing guard.

"Take your picture now, Isabella," Aunt Violeta said, her smile proud and wide.

Isa held up her camera and captured the iconic landmark.

*Got it.*

# CHAPTER 2

# THE WOMAN

The Rodriguez girls woke up the next morning to the smell of breakfast. When their aunt saw them, she ushered Isa and Marta to the dining room table where there were plates already set out on placemats. There were fancy napkins with silver rings around them. All of the silverware was nicely arranged.

"I'm starting to feel like royalty," Marta whispered.

Isa nodded. It really felt like their aunt was pulling out all the stops to make sure they were having the best visit ever. She wondered how it was going to feel to go back home in less than a week.

"I hope you two are hungry," Aunt Violeta said. She walked into the dining room with a plate of steaming pancakes in one hand and a bowl of strawberries in the other. Once she set them down, the girls each forked a flapjack onto their place setting as their aunt returned with a tray of scrambled eggs, chorizo, sliced ham, orange juice, maple syrup, and whipped cream.

"This is fantastic," Isa said, slapping some whipped

cream onto her pancake. "You don't have to do all of this for us, though, really."

"Yeah, we're used to a bowl of cereal or some frozen waffles back home," Marta said. "My mom is going to say you're spoiling us."

Aunt Violeta smiled and shrugged. "Ah, my sister doesn't need to know. Besides, these are special days," she said. "And I like to do special things for my special nieces."

Both Marta and Isa laughed, and a moment later, Aunt Violeta joined in.

"I said special too many times, didn't I?"

"You're *especially* good at using that word," Marta said before jabbing some eggs with her fork.

"I was thinking today is the perfect day for us to go to the beach," Aunt Violeta said. "Don't you think?"

Isa glanced out the window. The sun was already bright, and there wasn't a cloud in the sky.

"Isn't every day pretty much perfect out here?"

Aunt Violeta nodded. "It is, but we have our occasional bad days. Last January, it got down to around 55 degrees."

Marta dropped her fork. "You're kidding, right?" she said.

"What?" Aunt Violeta asked with a sly smile.

"You act like *that's* cold? You lived in Des Moines for pretty much your whole life! You've seen insane winters with two feet of snow on the ground."

"Fifty-five degrees isn't cold," Isa said in agreement.

"It's cold for here," Aunt Violeta protested. "Besides, when you live somewhere warm for a while, your body adjusts. I'm not used to those low temperatures anymore."

Isa shook her head. She could remember wearing shorts when it was in the fifties back home. She imagined people in Los Angeles bundling up when it got below 60 degrees.

*They really are weird out here,* she thought.

The three of them finished breakfast and worked together to clean up the kitchen. After brushing their teeth and digging out their swimsuits, they were back in the car and heading for the beach.

———

If Isa had any complaints about California, it had to be the traffic. It seemed like no matter where they went—and regardless of when they were on the road— there seemed to be cars everywhere. It made going anywhere in the city take a long time. She took pictures of the traffic along the way.

Good, bad, traffic . . . Isa wanted to remember it all.

"Have you girls ever heard of Route 66?" Aunt Violeta asked from the front seat.

"Isn't that some old song?" Marta replied.

Their aunt smiled and nodded.

"There is a song about it, yes," Aunt Violeta replied. "But it's more than that. It was a long stretch of road that was one of the originals when they started building interstate highways back in the old days."

Isa was pretty sure she'd heard the song Marta was talking about but couldn't remember how it went. There was something in the lyrics about "kicks."

"This isn't Route 66, is it, Aunt Violeta?" Isa asked. She looked at the road sign on the corner. It said "Santa Monica Boulevard."

"It is, smart girl," Aunt Violeta replied. "And we're just about at the end of it."

As they drove past the countless stores along Santa Monica Boulevard, Isa could see their trip was going to be worth it. There were more palm trees clustered around what looked like a park. Beyond that, she could see the sunlight shimmering on distant water.

*The Pacific Ocean,* Isa thought. She leaned forward in her seat as if to give herself a better view.

"Oh wow," Marta said, sounding genuine. "That's crazy."

It was the first time either of them had been to the ocean. There were a few lakes near where they lived in Iowa, but nothing as majestic and enormous as the sight they were seeing. The water seemed to stretch out forever, and even though the windows were up, Isa could almost hear the sounds of waves crashing against the sand.

"So if this is the end of Route 66, where does it start?" Isa asked, unable to take her eyes off the water.

"Chicago, Illinois," Aunt Violeta said proudly. "Back then, you could drive the two-thousand-plus miles from there and end up here. Santa Monica was the end of the line."

Marta looked puzzled.

"So you can't do it anymore?" she asked.

"Well, the roads have changed, so Route 66 doesn't actually exist as it once did," Aunt Violeta said. "But there's your history lesson for the day, and you can tell your friends back home you drove along Route 66 for a bit."

Both Isa and Marta looked out and saw a long pier with an amusement park at the end of it. There was a Ferris wheel, a roller coaster, and a bunch of other rides. Farther out in the water, they could see a few people surfing. Isa watched some guy fall off his board and into the ocean.

"Isn't there a beach out here somewhere where a bunch of muscle-heads lift weights?" Marta asked.

Aunt Violeta laughed.

"You're probably thinking of Venice Beach a little farther south," she replied. "There's an outdoor gym there."

They found a place to park in the already jammed parking lot and grabbed their beach towels, chairs, and umbrella. Isa listened and could hear the surf, smell the salt in the air, and hear the strange cooing of seagulls flying overhead.

Even though she was wearing flip-flops, Isa felt the heat from the parking lot's blacktop through the rubber. She'd been warned that Southern California in July got really hot, and they were right.

The three of them set up camp close to the water but far enough away to avoid the waves crashing in. They applied plenty of sunscreen and waited a few minutes for it to soak in.

"I'm totally going into the water," Marta said after a while.

Isa wanted to take some more pictures. It felt like no matter where she turned, she saw something else she wanted to capture.

She watched as her older sister ran off toward the waves.

"Are you going into the water too, Isabella?"

Isa shrugged. "Is it safe? I thought I heard there were sharks out there."

Aunt Violeta nodded. "Well, there are definitely sharks in the ocean, but you knew that already."

"But here?"

"There are sharks out there, but the odds of being attacked by one are very slim," Aunt Violeta said. "They go where there is easy food to eat."

*People would be easy for them to eat,* Isa thought. She looked out and watched Marta splashing around in the waves.

"I read an article that said you're more likely to risk life and limb eating a hot dog than swimming in the ocean," Aunt Violeta said.

Isa smiled. She'd heard about what was in hot dogs.

"I might wait awhile," Isa said. "Just enjoy the scenery for a minute or two."

They watched Marta get nearly knocked over by a wave but quickly straighten herself up and wipe the wet hair out of her face. She turned and gave a thumbs-up to Isa and her aunt.

*I wish I were as brave as she is*, Isa thought. *She never worries about stuff like sharks or drowning or anything.*

Isa lined up her shot and took a picture of her older, adventurous sister. The ocean made her look tiny in comparison.

"You've been taking a lot of pictures," Aunt Violeta said. "Get any good ones so far?"

Isa nodded, excited to share her passion with someone. She always caught a lot of grief from Marta about living in the now and experiencing the world, instead of capturing it.

She switched to playback mode on her camera and scrolled through the images. Seeing that her aunt was interested and leaned in to take a look, Isa took her through a virtual tour of the photos, starting with Marta and her at the airport, waiting to board the plane. She showed her aunt a shot of the clouds from her window seat in the air, their first palm tree, and a selfie of all of them together when Aunt Violeta had picked them up.

"Oh," Aunt Violeta said. "Send that one to me!"

Isa clicked through all of them, one after another, until they were caught up to the present. When they reached the end, her aunt rubbed her back a few times.

"You've got a great eye, Isabella," she said. "At four-teen, you've already got the makings of a talented photographer."

Isa blushed. "Thanks!"

Marta called for the two of them from the water.

"C'mon!" she shouted. "This is amazing!"

Isa looked at her aunt, who nodded toward the ocean.

"What do you think?"

"Maybe in a minute," Isa said.

"See you out there, then."

Isa watched her aunt join her sister, then turned her attention to her photos again.

*Does Aunt Violeta really think I'm talented?* She wondered. *Or is she just saying that because she's my aunt and she's supposed to say that kind of thing?*

As she clicked through some of her "greatest hits," she stopped at the photo she had taken the night before when they'd arrived at their aunt's house. It was the one of the Hollywood sign she had captured from the balcony on the back of Aunt Violeta's house.

It was a really great shot, framed up well to show how ginormous the letters really were.

As Isa was about to click to the next photo, something

caught her eye. There, atop the letter H, she saw a shadowy shape. She zoomed in and then used the left arrow button to line it up to the center and zoomed in some more.

*What is that?* Isa asked herself. *Is that a person up there?*

She studied the image a little more closely. It looked like a woman standing on top of the left side of the H. Since the woman was so far away from where Isa had taken the picture, she couldn't make out any details other than the woman's clothing. To Isa, it looked like she was wearing a glamorous dress and had long hair pinned up in spots. The face, however, was totally obscured.

*Was there really someone up there?*

She zoomed back out and saw that the woman was nothing more than a tiny blip in the picture and was amazed she had even noticed it. Since she'd learned that most photographers took a couple of pictures in a row, she flipped to the next one she had of the Hollywood sign.

Isa zoomed in again and saw that the woman wasn't in the next shot.

She flipped back, and there she was again, back on top of the H.

Isa's heart began to beat a little more quickly. She couldn't imagine being up that high. The view would be amazing but not worth risking your life for.

*Who is she?* Isa wondered. *And why was she up there?*

As she stared at the photo for a few more moments, a frightening thought occurred to her as she flipped to the next picture: *And what happened to her?*

# CHAPTER 3

# HILL HIKE

When her sister and aunt came back from the ocean, Isa could hardly wait to show them what she found.

"You need to see this," Isa insisted, holding up her camera.

"Seriously," Marta said. "You can't take a day off from being a shutterbug? And are you really not going to go in the ocean?"

Isa looked past them at the breaking waves and saw a trio of surfers paddling out to sea. A little boy was building a sandcastle quickly and clapping any time the water washed parts of it away.

"Maybe next time," Isa said.

"Is there going to be a next time?" Marta asked, directing her question to her aunt.

Aunt Violeta nodded. "Of course," she said. "We can come to the beach every day if you girls want. It's our week—we make the rules!"

Both Isa and Marta smiled. Isa liked the sound of that.

"Well, good," Marta replied. "Fine, show us what you have."

Isa turned her camera to show them the picture she had taken of the Hollywood sign. Both her aunt and sister leaned in to see what Isa had captured.

"Look," Isa said. "You see that?"

Marta took the camera and held it close to her face. When that didn't seem to do the trick, she made a frame around the screen with her hand to block out the sun.

"Yeah, there's a little speck or something on the screen," Marta said. "It's a piece of sand, sis."

"Look on the top of the H," Isa insisted.

There was silence for a moment, and she waited for her sister to cry out in amazement or horror at what Isa'd managed to catch with her camera.

"It looks like a little dot or something," Marta said.

"Zoom in," Isa urged.

Her aunt turned to her and asked in a whisper, "What is it?"

Isa shook her head. "I want you to see for yourself," she said. "Or maybe I just imagined it."

Marta sighed and handed the camera back to her sister. "I don't see anything," she said with a shrug.

Isa was baffled. *How can she not see it? There's clearly a woman standing up there!*

Her aunt took the camera from her hand and, with Isa's help, zoomed in on the top of the letter H as far as it would go. Isa watched as her aunt's eyebrows went up a few times as if puzzled by what she was seeing.

"Do you see it?" Isa asked.

"It looks like something, sweetheart," Aunt Violeta said. "But it's hard to tell what it is. Maybe it's the sun or . . ."

Isa couldn't stand it anymore.

"It's a person," she blurted. "There was a person standing on top of the H, and then, in the next picture, she's gone!"

Marta looked at her younger sister like she'd just dropped out of the sky.

"Wow, take it easy," she said. "It didn't look like anything to me. No need to get all—"

"You can't tell me that doesn't look like some woman in a dress standing up there," Isa said, interrupting her. "And then the next shot? She's gone."

"Probably a speck of dust or something on the lens," Marta said. "I mean, why would anyone be up there?"

Aunt Violeta squinted at the photo again.

"It does look a little like a person, I guess," she said.

It made Isa feel like her aunt was just saying that to calm her down. Isa appreciated it, but she didn't like feeling like Aunt Violeta was telling her what she wanted to hear.

"Can you see what I mean?" Isa asked.

"Yes, yes," Aunt Violeta said, nodding. "It is very peculiar. It could be a daredevil or some kids messing around. This is Los Angeles, after all."

Isa took her camera back and looked at the picture one more time before turning it off.

*Neither of them believe me*, she thought, then realized they didn't have to. *I know what I saw!*

---

After lunch at a not-so-fancy place (at the insistence of Isa and Marta), the three of them headed home. Isa caught her sister pretty much falling asleep in the car on the way back. All the sun and running around the city must have sapped her energy.

When they got back to the Hollywood Hills, both Marta and Aunt Violeta decided to take naps. Within a few minutes, the two of them had retired to their rooms, and Isa was left on her own in the quiet space of her aunt's house.

She wandered around inside a bit, then tried to see if there was something on TV to watch but didn't find anything interesting. Turned out, daytime television in the summer was just as bad on the West Coast as it was in the Midwest. After skimming somewhere around three hundred channels, Isa turned the television off and glanced out the window.

She glanced up at the Hollywood sign and tried to see if she could see anyone or anything on top of the H or any of the other letters.

Realizing she was getting a little stir-crazy, Isa decided she would try to hike up the hill and take some pictures from the base of the sign.

She found a bottle of water in the refrigerator, borrowed a sun visor from her aunt's closet, along with a backpack, and put on a sturdy pair of walking shoes. Judging by the hill's slope, she didn't think her sandy pair of flip-flops would cut it. She wrote a note to tell her aunt and sister where she was going. Then, grabbing her precious camera, she slung it around her neck.

Isa was ready for her adventure.

Being careful to close the door quietly, she left for her hike up Mount Lee.

The journey up the hill was far more difficult than Isa imagined. The ground was rocky and cluttered with thorny little bushes that grew along the man-made trails.

More than a few times, Isa felt her footing slip, making her pretty sure she might twist her ankle. On top of that, it was incredibly hot with no real trees to provide shade from the punishing sun.

Isa stopped when she found a place with good footholds and pulled her water bottle out of the backpack to pause for a drink. The water had quickly gotten warm in the hour or so she'd been hiking, but it didn't matter. She was thirsty.

The air smelled strange being so high above the city. It had a real chemical stink to it. Looking back over the neighborhood and downtown Hollywood, she could see that the sky had a yellowish tint.

Isa had read about smog and how the pollution from so many cars caused it. It was strange to think it was a cloud of chemical stuff sort of stuck in the air.

Something shifted in the gritty ground nearby, and she could swear she could hear a rapid clicking sound.

*Snake!* Isa thought and moved quickly up the slope.

"So maybe this is a dumb idea," Isa said aloud.

She glanced down to where she'd just stood. She expected to see a rattlesnake twist its way across the trail, but nothing happened. It made her think that maybe she'd gotten just a little too close to its home and had been given a warning.

She looked up and saw the sign almost towering above her.

"Whoa," she whispered and took some pictures. Isa framed the photo to try and get as many of the letters in as she could. She even turned around and took some shots of the tiny houses below and the city that seemed to stretch out forever.

There was no getting around it, Los Angeles was *huge.*

She looked back at her pictures, mostly satisfied with what she had gotten. No one in her school's photography club was going to get pictures like the ones she'd taken. But Isa wanted to get even closer. She decided to continue up the slope.

It was steeper the farther along she got. And in some of the more slippery sections, she forced herself to almost bend forward and crawl up. When the ground leveled out again, she realized she was about as far as she could get.

The sign's H and O stood like giants above her.

Isa aimed her camera at the letters. As she did, she saw a face peer down at her from the H.

*What is that?*

As if on instinct, she moved the camera away and felt her feet slide beneath her a little. She slid backward, scraping her knees against the sharp, hot rocks. Ignoring the pain and the small dots of blood that welled up through her dusty skin, Isa looked up.

There was no one there.

*I saw her,* Isa thought.

She instantly realized it was the woman she'd captured with her distant photo from her aunt's balcony.

*Who is she? What is she doing on top of the H?*

"Hello?" Isa called. "Is someone up there?"

There was no answer, but a hot wind blew across the hill, kicking up dust in a small cloud.

Isa waited to say anything else. Maybe it was someone hiding up there, and Isa had startled her. Either way, she wanted to know, even if it wasn't any of her business in the first place.

"Can you hear me?" Isa's voice sounded small against the majesty of the sign and the enormity of the world below her.

Again, silence.

Isa looked through her camera again and aimed it up at the H. There didn't appear to be anyone up there—no woman, no face. Nothing but blue sky up above with the tiniest, wispiest cloud drifting past.

And then . . .

. . . what looked like a hand hanging over the edge.

Isa instinctively took a picture and then looked with her own eyes to see if she could see it. There was no hand, just the bright white surface of the first letter of

California's most famous sign. She glanced through the camera's viewfinder again and saw the hand was gone too.

*What is going on?* Isa's heart started working up from a light jog to a steadier run.

She thought about calling her aunt and sister to wake them up but wasn't sure what good that would do.

Isa began to wonder if maybe the sun was getting to her. She'd heard that people who were overly hot could get heatstroke. It made you feel sick and see things that weren't there.

*I don't feel sick*, Isa thought. *I'm hot, but I feel fine. Just a little sweaty and scraped up.*

She looked around at the dried-out bushes and chunks of rock that made up the hill. Nothing there seemed out of the ordinary. She wasn't seeing or hearing anything strange in the other places she looked. It wasn't like she was a nurse or a doctor, but she was pretty sure she didn't have heatstroke.

There was just something weird about the Hollywood Hills, and she wanted to know what it was.

*You're scared of sharks and going into the ocean*, Isa told herself. *But you're okay climbing a mountain crawling with snakes to take pictures and talk with a creepy woman who would prefer to remain hidden. Maybe you are weird, Isabella Rodriguez.*

Isa considered calling out to the woman hiding up on the sign one more time before heading back. As she did, she glanced up to the huge letter and saw with her own two eyes a woman standing on top of the letter.

# CHAPTER 4

# EDGE OF THE H

Isa gasped, feeling like she'd gotten the wind knocked out of her. She had to double-check to make sure she wasn't just seeing things. She closed her eyes for a few seconds and opened them again, half expecting to see that the woman had hidden herself or disappeared.

She was still there.

As Isa got her breathing under control, she studied the woman standing above her. She looked . . . different. She seemed almost faded, like something left out in the sun for too long. It was hard to make out any distinct colors on the dress or the shoes she wore. Her hair was lighter colored, maybe blond.

It made Isa nervous to see how close to the edge of the H she stood.

"Hello?" Isa called, her voice sounding smaller than ever beneath the mammoth letter and great wide-open space.

The woman didn't respond. She seemed to look back behind her and nodded once as if talking to someone

Isa couldn't see. After a moment, she faced forward again and put her hand up as if she were talking or . . .

*Singing.*

Goosebumps dotted her arms as she realized something: She couldn't hear the woman singing at all. There was no noise coming from the top of the H. Isa wasn't sure if it was because of the wind or how high up the woman was. She could only hear the wind blowing through the dry scrub grass and the pounding of her heart.

"Hey!" Isa called again. "Please be careful up there!"

She couldn't change how shaky her voice was, and she knew it was because she was scared. Something was off about the woman and the entire situation.

*Maybe she can't see me*, Isa thought. She walked back down the slope a bit so that there was another thirty yards between her and where the woman stood. Small rocks scraped loose from under Isa's feet tumbled down the hill. She knew a bad step would send her falling too.

When Isa turned around to face the sign once more, she fully expected the woman to have disappeared again.

But the woman was still up there, looking out over Hollywood. Though the wind was blowing across the

hills, kicking up dirt, Isa noticed that the woman's dress didn't appear to move much at all.

"Hello?" Isa called. "Can you see me? I'm down here!"

The woman didn't seem to notice or hear her.

Thankful she'd thought to wear the visor, Isa looked up at the H and tried to see more details about the woman. Though it was hard to tell, it looked like the woman's mouth was moving, but Isa couldn't hear her voice.

*I should be able to hear her.* Isa's heartbeat quickened. *What is she doing?*

She watched the woman for a little longer, waiting for something to happen—for the woman to climb down, to notice her . . . anything. When nothing changed, Isa carefully raised her camera.

With shaky hands, she lined up the shot and took the photo. She quickly pulled the image up and looked at the picture she'd taken. There was no denying that there was a woman standing on the Hollywood sign.

Not even Marta could deny it.

Isa held the camera up again and zoomed in as close as she could to the woman's face. It was hard to make out the details. She could see her eyes, nose, and mouth, but they seemed blurred, as if she were standing behind a smudged window.

Even so, Isa took another picture. Then another.

As she lowered her camera, something horrible happened.

The woman fell.

Isa turned as she saw the woman drop from the giant letter H. She squeezed her eyes shut and let go of her camera. It banged against her chest as she covered her ears.

She expected to hear a scream through her hands or the heavy sound of a body hitting the hill, but she heard nothing. It reminded her of watching a movie with the sound completely turned off. Everything was different when it was silent.

Isa was breathing heavily, as if she'd just run up and down the hill twice with no stopping. Her chest rose and fell, and she slowly removed her hands from her ears. She didn't open her eyes yet. She couldn't.

In the valley below, she could hear the sound of a car horn honking. An airplane flew overhead. She didn't hear any anguished cries or anything from the place where the woman must have landed.

*I can't look*, Isa thought. *I can't look, but I have to*

*look. What if she needs help? Shouldn't I call the police or an ambulance?*

Isa made a deal with herself: She would peek out through her eyelids very slowly. If she saw something horrible, she'd close her eyes, turn her back, and call 911.

She turned back toward the sign. "One, two . . ." Isa whispered to herself. On "three," she opened her eyes to a thin slit and peeked out.

There was nothing in the spot where the woman would've landed. She turned her head to the right. Nothing there either. She steered her gaze in the other direction and found nothing but bright, rocky ground and sparse plants.

By then, Isa's eyes were fully open. Relief mixed with confusion washed over her. She was glad there wasn't a dead body lying in a heap nearby but couldn't quite understand why there wasn't.

*I saw her,* Isa thought, scanning the hills for any sign of the mysterious woman. *I know I saw her fall. I couldn't have just imagined it.*

Isa took a few cautious steps forward, looking to the left and right.

"Hello?" she called. "Are you okay?"

As she suspected, there was no answer.

Isa carefully climbed up a little higher, approaching the spot on the hill where the woman would have likely landed. As she got close, she felt the sweat along her brow and around her neck start to cool. It was as if someone had splashed cold water onto her, and it made her shiver slightly.

She glanced up at the sky and could see the sun was still out, burning the side of the hill with all of its solar force.

Just when she thought her hillside hike couldn't get any stranger, a flowery scent drifted past her nose. It was sweet and strong and unlike anything she'd smelled since starting her trek up to the sign.

"It smells like perfume," Isa realized out loud.

The more she sniffed the air, the more obvious it became. She wasn't smelling some hidden hill flowers but an artificial scent that reminded her of something her grandma might wear.

*Was the woman wearing perfume? Is she close by?*

Isa listened intently. Even if the woman were nearby, Isa suspected she would've heard the woman's cries for help or heard her moving through the gritty ground. Isa didn't hear anything.

"I don't get it," Isa whispered to herself.

She glanced once more up at the huge letters. There were no more faces or women or anything else. The signs made a metallic squeak as a strong wind whipped against the stark white surfaces.

Unsure of what else she could do, Isa took more photos of the surrounding area. She knew she'd want to share what she'd encountered with her sister and her aunt. She thought completely documenting the scene would help her tell the story.

Isa took a picture of the framework that the letters were attached to. She photographed the area just below the letters where she assumed the woman would've hit the ground. For a visual reference of where she was standing, she shot the HOLL part of the sign.

After a few moments, the cold sensations she'd felt had passed, making her wonder how or why that had happened in the first place. Nothing seemed to make sense, which made Isa wonder if maybe she truly *was* suffering from heatstroke after all.

She lowered her camera and took another few sips of water from her bottle. As she did, she saw something moving to her right.

Isa jumped and dropped her water. Before she could

reach down to grab it, it rolled down the hill, spilling its contents along the way, leaving a thin, watery trail.

She turned and looked to her right, scanning the brush and hill for any sort of movement.

*Is it another snake?*

"Is someone there?" Isa called. "Please don't hide from me. I'm not dangerous or anything."

She waited for an answer but wasn't surprised when she didn't hear one. Whoever the woman was, if she really was there at all, she didn't seem to be in the mood to talk.

"I took your picture," Isa said. "I saw you on top of the H and . . ."

A cold feeling washed over her again. It was different than the feeling of her sweat cooling on her face. This time, it felt like she'd stepped outside in Des Moines in the middle of January. Her goose bumps instantly returned, and the bones inside her body felt like they'd been dipped in a cooler full of ice.

Even worse was the unmistakable sensation that she was being watched.

*I need to get out of here*, Isa decided. Something was very wrong with the Hollywood Hills, and the situation seemed to be getting stranger with every second. Her scraped knee throbbed in agreement.

Isa turned and scrambled down the hill, slowing down when it felt like she was losing her footing. Gravel and rocks tumbled ahead of her, bouncing down the slope. After a moment, the icy feeling she experienced had passed again. As it did, she thought she could hear a whisper in the wind.

*"Waiiii . . ."*

Isa's heart drummed more quickly, panic rising in her throat with every passing second. She grabbed her camera to prevent it from bouncing, then broke into a run. On the way down, she caught a quick glint on the ground and bent to pick up her empty plastic water bottle.

Scared or not scared, she didn't want to litter.

Isa didn't even think about slowing until the hill started to level out into a more easy-to-navigate terrain. Even so, she ran ahead, heading into the neighborhood on Mulholland Drive at the base of Mount Lee.

She ran through the street, looking for her aunt's house. Her knees felt hot and stingy as dirt and sweat mixed into the scrapes, but Isa kept running and never looked back.

# CHAPTER 5

# UNEXPLAINABLE

Isa burst through the front door of her aunt's house, slamming it behind her. She'd completely forgotten that her aunt and sister were in their rooms, taking a nap.

*Someone was watching me*, Isa thought. Her mind was still reeling from all that had happened in the last hour or so. *And I heard something. A voice or someone crying.*

There was the creak of a door down the hallway, and Isa nearly cried out in terror. She stood in the entryway, and a dark shape moved through the doorway and into the kitchen.

"Is everything okay, Isabella?" her aunt said. She was draped in a dark-grey bathrobe, and her eyes were sleepy and half open as if she'd just woken up.

Isa nodded, still out of breath from her long run down the side of the hill and through the neighborhood. She let air out slowly, trying her best to calm down.

"Oh my," Aunt Violeta said, tightening the belt of her robe. "What's happened to you?"

Her aunt came through the kitchen and into the front entryway toward Isa. As she did, her tired eyes widened as she looked Isa up and down. When she caught a look at Isa's scraped knees, she looked downright horrified.

"You're hurt!"

Isa glanced down at her knees. There were small rivulets of blood from the little scrapes she'd sustained, but they didn't even bother her all that much. She pulled off the visor, unshouldered her backpack, and set the empty water bottle down.

"How did this happen?" Aunt Violeta asked, her hand creeping up to her mouth as if to hold back any further gasps.

"I took a hike up into the hills to get closer to the Hollywood sign," Isa replied, finally able to put words together and talk. "I slipped and scraped up my knees a little, but—"

"It's dangerous up there," her aunt interrupted. "Oh my word, look at your poor legs, Isabella!"

"I'm okay," Isa said. "I'm just—"

"Come, come," her aunt said. "Let's get you cleaned up right away."

Aunt Violeta walked her into the kitchen and had her sit down at the table, moving her slowly as if to prevent further injuries. Isa took her camera off and set it on the table beside her.

Before Isa could say anything more, her aunt disappeared down the hallway and came back with a first aid kit. It looked like something from the 1980s, but after she set it down and opened the yellowed case, Isa could see it was stocked with fresh supplies.

Aunt Violeta pulled out some gauze, a few bandages, and a tube of antibacterial cream. After setting everything down, she dashed back into the hallway and returned with a white washcloth. She quickly ran the washcloth under the sink in the kitchen and came over to Isa. She pulled a chair over and sat down in front of her niece.

"Okay," Aunt Violeta said. "Let me see."

Isa lifted her right leg up first, keeping the knee bent. She knew what was coming, and it was pretty much the worst part. Her aunt was going to run that washcloth across her knees to clean it off.

"I think it looks worse than it actually is," Isa said, already wincing in anticipation.

"Let's hope so," Aunt Violeta said. Then she murmured under her breath, "My sister will flip her lid if I send you home hurt."

Isa closed her eyes as her aunt gently wiped the dust and blood from her knees. It felt strange at age fourteen to have someone help clean her up, but she appreciated it. The scrapes weren't as bad as they looked, which seemed to make Aunt Violeta breathe a little easier.

It actually felt good to have the cream smeared onto the small little cuts. As her aunt placed the last bandage over her wounds, Marta came into the kitchen.

"What's going on out here?" she asked sleepily.

Before Isa could respond, her aunt did for her.

"Your sister went on a little adventure while we had our siesta," Aunt Violeta replied, shaking her head. "You should've seen how dirty her legs were. I'm not sure she left much dust up there!"

As Marta came around to take a look at the damage, Isa reached for her camera.

"It was crazy up there," Isa said.

"Those letters are enormous, aren't they?" Aunt Violeta remarked.

"Well, yeah," Isa said. "But some even stranger things happened—stuff I don't even think I can explain."

Marta twisted her mouth up like she'd just bitten into a particularly sour lemon.

"Oh, here we go."

Isa ignored her and grabbed her camera. She clicked through the pictures until she got to the first one.

"Remember that woman from the picture I took yesterday?" Isa asked. "The one on top of the Hollywood sign?"

"I'm still not sure that was a woman," Marta said. "But go on."

"She was up there again!" Isa cried. "And I got a better picture of her!"

Isa turned the camera around and thrust it out for the two women to see. She waited for their reaction, prepared for them to cry out and tell her that it was creepy or something. Anything.

"Huh? I don't see it," Marta said.

"Is that the right picture, Isabella?" Aunt Violeta asked. "I'm not sure that's . . ."

Isa quickly turned the camera around and looked

at the picture. It was a shot looking straight up at the H, but unlike the photo she'd taken and seen on the hillside, there was no woman standing on top of the letter.

"This doesn't make any sense," Isa whispered, more to herself than to her captive audience.

"Too much time out in the sun," Marta said. She took a step away as if she meant to find something else to do than waste her time looking at Isa's photo collection.

Isa frantically clicked through the other pictures she had taken, looking for any sign of the woman she'd captured. None of them had the woman's image or anything resembling a person. Just a bunch of big white letters, blue sky, and the sun-scorched hillside.

*I saw her*, Isa thought, feeling her face flush red with embarrassment. *I know I saw her!*

"Can I take a look, dear?" Aunt Violeta asked. She was talking to Isa in a gentle voice, like she was trying to make her feel better. Isa appreciated the gesture but didn't want anyone to feel sorry for her.

"Yeah," Isa said, handing the camera over. "Sure."

She sat back in her chair while Marta rummaged through the cabinets, likely looking for something to snack on.

"Do you have any chips or anything, Aunt Violeta?"

Marta asked from the other side of the kitchen's large island.

"There are some kale chips in the cupboard next to the microwave," Aunt Violeta replied without looking up from the camera.

"Oh okay," Marta said. "Never mind."

Isa watched her aunt as she looked through the photos. Her eyebrows were furrowed, a sign that she was really concentrating.

*Did she find the falling woman?*

"What are you seeing?" Isa asked. "Anything? Do you see her?"

Aunt Violeta shook her head and blinked a few times as if trying to clear her eyes for a fresh look at the photographs.

"I don't see the lady you were talking about," Aunt Violeta admitted. "But look at this."

Her aunt handed her the camera and moved in close so the two of them could look together. Isa looked at the photo. It was one she'd taken at the base of the hill in an attempt to capture the entire sign before she was too close to fit all nine letters into the frame.

To make it look better, she'd left some room to the left of the H and to the right of the D. Isa thought it was almost postcard-worthy.

"I don't see anything," Isa said. "Where am I supposed to be looking?"

Aunt Violeta pointed her finger to the space next to the letter D on the far right of the photo.

Isa stared at the space, and her eyes widened. If she didn't know any better, it looked like . . .

"Is that the letter L?" Isa asked.

Her aunt nodded.

Isa stared at the photo. The letter was faded, almost to the point of being invisible. Her aunt pointed to the sliver of green next to the nearly transparent L.

"And look at that," Aunt Violeta said.

They both stared. There was part of another letter there, an angular one that could really only be one letter.

"Part of an A," Isa whispered, shaking her head.

*A faded woman, nearly invisible letters*, she thought. *What is going on up in those hills?*

All of the letters, even the hidden ones, were roughly the same size. They almost looked like phantoms of something that used to be there.

"Hollywoodla," Isa said. "It doesn't make sense. The sign says *Hollywood*."

Her aunt sat back in her chair with a creak. "Actually," she said, "there used to be more letters a long time ago."

Isa looked up from the camera to study her aunt's face. She thought maybe this was some sort of joke but could see that Aunt Violeta was serious. If Isa wasn't mistaken, her aunt looked creeped out.

"Really?" Isa had never heard that. "What did it say?"

"Hollywoodland," Aunt Violeta said. "The sign was originally built as an advertisement for a real-estate development of the same name, I think. Sometime in the 1940s, they decided to leave the 'land' off of it due to costs for repairs and maintenance."

"If the letters have been gone for"—Isa did some quick calculating in her head—"around eighty years or so, why are they showing up in my photo?"

"I'm not sure," Aunt Violeta said and glanced toward the big windows that looked off to the hills.

"Are you guys still looking for the lady who's not there?" Marta called from the living room along the back of the house.

*The lady who's not there?* Isa thought, her sister's words repeating in her head.

The two of them didn't answer Marta. Instead, Isa stood up and felt her slightly shredded knees sting momentarily. She walked to the window and looked out over the balcony and up at the letters. She stared at the sign to try and see where the L, A, N, and D would've been, once upon a time.

There weren't any letters there anymore, not even the phantoms of them like she'd seen in her picture. As she continued to stare, a cold shiver ran through her, as if she were standing beneath an air-conditioning vent.

Aunt Violeta joined her and stared up at the sign too.

"I'm beginning to think I'm seeing and imagining things," Isa admitted. "Up in the hills, I could see that woman. I could hear a voice. I could even . . ."

Her aunt looked at Isa as her words trailed off.

"What, Isabella?" Aunt Violeta asked.

"I could smell perfume or something," Isa said quietly.

"Strange," her aunt said. "Very, very strange. Do you remember what this woman looked like?"

Isa looked at her camera and sifted through a few more pictures, hoping to jog her memory. It was hard to remember, especially since the woman appeared almost as if she were a shadow, which Isa knew didn't make much sense.

As she clicked to the last picture she had taken, she recognized it as a picture of the sign's base, just below the second L.

There was something there.

Isa felt her heart begin to rumble in her ribs. She zoomed in closer to one of the supports that helped keep the letters affixed to the side of the hill.

She could see a face. It was the woman, peering back at her from beneath the sign.

"The lady looked exactly like this," Isa said, showing her aunt the camera with shaky hands.

# CHAPTER 6

# SEVENTEEN

Isa half expected the image of the woman to not show up and for her aunt to say, "What am I looking at, Isabella? I don't see anything."

That didn't happen.

"Oh," Aunt Violeta said as she looked at the photo. "Oh my."

Her aunt took the camera from Isa's hand and looked at it more closely. Isa looked over her aunt's shoulder as they studied the image she'd captured.

"I'm not just seeing things, am I?" Isa asked.

"No," Aunt Violeta whispered. "Because I'm seeing it too, sweetheart."

Isa looked at the woman. She wore a full-length dress that looked like it had been in fashion a long time ago. Her light-blond hair was curled slightly and hung just below her shoulders. Though the details were hazy, her eyes looked wide and expressive, as if she had been just as scared as Isa felt now.

"You didn't see her when you were up there?" Aunt Violeta asked.

"Well, I did, but then she fell," Isa replied.

"What?" her aunt asked. "What do you mean she fell?"

"She was standing on top of the H, just like I saw yesterday," Isa explained. "When I got up close to the sign, I could see her standing up there. It looked like she was saying something. I couldn't hear her though."

Isa paused, thinking back to what she'd seen and what had happened.

"Then, suddenly, she fell off," Isa said.

"You saw her fall?" Aunt Violeta's eyes were wide with shock.

"Yes," Isa said. "But I closed my eyes and covered my ears so I didn't see or hear her land. I didn't want to watch that."

Her aunt looked upset, as if she were imagining what a fall like that could do to a person.

"That's terrible," Aunt Violeta said. "And I don't blame you."

Isa took a deep breath. "When I finally looked, there was nothing there."

She watched her aunt click away from the photo of the woman hiding beneath the supports. Her eyes scanned the others while her head shook back and forth.

"I called for her and looked around, but I never saw her again," Isa said. "Until you spotted her in that photo. It's weird, right?"

"Yes," Aunt Violeta agreed. "But I think I know what it is."

Isa felt her breath hitch momentarily.

"I think you've captured an image of a ghost," Aunt Violeta said.

"What?!" Isa cried and reached for her camera. "No way. Are you serious?"

Her aunt nodded.

"I've heard stories that the hills were haunted," Aunt Violeta said. "But I guess I never really believed them."

Isa wasn't sure what she believed. There were enough TV shows about ghosts, so she guessed there might be *something* to it. Before then, she'd never really thought much about scary stuff like that.

She stared at the woman in the picture. It looked like a real person but different somehow. Hazy, faded . . . not really there.

Marta, likely feeling as if she were missing out on something, came over and joined them at the window.

"What are you guys talking about?"

"Aunt Violeta thinks I caught a picture of a ghost," Isa said.

"Let me see," Marta said, rolling her eyes and reaching for the camera.

There was barely a pause before Marta cried out and threw the camera across the room in shock. To Isa's relief, it landed safely on her aunt's sectional, next to the faux-fur pillows.

"Are you kidding me?!" Marta shouted.

"Are you kidding *me*?!" Isa shouted back. "You threw my camera!"

Isa went to collect her camera and checked to make sure it was okay. Everything looked fine, and the picture of the ghost lady was right where Isa had left her.

After Isa and her aunt caught Marta up on what they'd seen, including the phantom letters on the Hollywood Hills, all three of them were staring out the window and up the hill. It was as if they were watching and waiting for a big storm to roll in.

"I'm almost afraid to go outside now," Marta said.

"Yeah," Isa said. "What do we do?"

"I'm not sure there's anything we can do," Aunt Violeta said. "I think you just caught something rare and amazing. Not sure there's much more to it than that."

"I wish we knew who she was," Isa said. "Like, what happened to her."

"I just want to know if she's going to try and get us," Marta shivered. "Oh wow. I just gave myself chills."

Isa watched her sister rub her arms up and down as if trying to warm herself.

"Do you think she will?" Isa asked, turning to her aunt.

Aunt Violeta shook her head and laughed. "I don't think so," she replied. "I've lived here for years and have never felt any sort of danger, paranormal or otherwise.

You just caught a snapshot of another time through your pictures, Isabella."

*A snapshot in time*, Isa thought. Somehow, that made her feel better and a lot less scared.

———————

The three of them sat around the swimming pool, just enjoying the weather. After a while, Isa felt worn out from her day's adventures.

"You look like you're ready to collapse," Aunt Violeta said.

"I could totally fall asleep," Isa said. Her eyes felt heavy and half open.

Marta turned from where she was dangling her feet in the pool.

"I can't recommend a nap enough," Marta said. "I feel like half a million dollars."

"Not a full million, Martalina?" Aunt Violeta asked before taking a sip of her iced tea.

"I would've if Isa hadn't woken me up earlier, slamming the door."

Isa kicked a nearby beach ball in her sister's direction.

"I was freaked out!" Isa cried. "You would've run right through the door to get away."

"Oh, whatever," Marta said, knocking the ball into the water.

Rather than continue to sit by the pool and let her head dip in half-asleep exhaustion, Isa excused herself and went into the house, heading straight for her room. She didn't bother to pull the covers back and, instead, flopped onto the bed face-first. After thirty seconds, she was sound asleep.

———————

Isa wasn't sure what time it was when she woke up. She didn't know where her phone was, and there weren't any other clocks in the bedroom. The sun was quite a bit lower in the sky, casting an almost-orange glow through the closed white mini-blinds.

Isa rubbed her arms. She was cold. Really cold.

It almost felt like she was inside of a walk-in freezer with the door closed. Isa knew the air conditioner was on around the clock. But this was a completely different kind of cold. Her bones felt encased in ice.

She brushed the hair out of her face and shivered. When she exhaled, she could see her breath.

"Hello?" Isa called. "Marta? Aunt Violeta?"

There was no answer.

Isa hopped off of her bed and felt that the ground was cold beneath her feet too.

*What is going on with the house?* she wondered. Then, *where are they?*

Assuming she'd find her aunt and sister still out on the patio, Isa quickly tiptoed over to her suitcase, fished out a pair of socks, and pulled them on.

The thin cotton socks helped a little bit but not much. She could still feel dull icy throbs on the bottom of her feet. She breathed out again, still surprised she could see her breath in wispy clouds on the air.

Isa walked into the hallway. It wasn't nearly as cold there, making her wonder if maybe there was just something wrong with her room. Maybe all of the air conditioning was being piped in there by mistake?

Isa moved from the hallway to the kitchen and glanced out across the living room to the sliding door that led to the balcony. Neither Marta nor her aunt were outside.

To make sure they weren't in the pool, Isa walked into the living room and past her aunt's large flat-screen TV. The pool was mostly still. No one had been in it to make waves in quite some time.

"Where did they go?" Isa wondered aloud, staring

out the window. As she was about to turn to look else-where, she caught a glimpse of movement in the glass.

There was someone behind her. She turned around to look.

"Marta?" Isa called.

No one answered.

"Marta," Isa said, her voice sounding irritated. "If you're trying to scare me, it's not funny."

Not wanting to let her sister surprise her, Isa turned around. There was no one in the living room or the kitchen.

"Aunt Violeta?"

Isa knew her aunt wouldn't do anything to scare her. She listened, hoping to hear her aunt answer.

She didn't.

If her aunt and sister weren't in the house, who had she seen?

Isa took a few cautious steps toward the center is-land in the kitchen. There, she could see that someone had brought her phone and camera inside and set them there. She also saw a blue sticky note.

She glanced over her shoulder to make sure some-one wasn't sneaking up behind her. She could feel her heart beat a little faster with each passing second.

When she got to the island, she glanced at the sticky note stuck to the marble countertop. She recognized her aunt's fancy writing. The note said:

*Isabella,*

*We didn't want to wake you. Marta and I went to pick up dinner for tonight. Thought we might stay in and watch a movie. Be back soon!*

*Hugs, Aunt Violeta.*

Isa looked over at her phone and touched the HOME button. The screen stayed dark. A moment later, the PLEASE RECHARGE symbol illuminated, letting her know her phone was completely dead.

"Perfect," Isa whispered. *Now I can't even call to see when they'll be back.*

Just then, she saw a parade of headlights run along the wall. Hoping it was her sister and aunt, already back from their food run, she headed back to her room to get her charging cable. Even in the doorway, she felt the cold emanating from inside the bedroom.

As she took a cautious step into the room, she felt like she was being watched. She waited a moment while her eyes adjusted to the dim light. Isa gasped. There, standing in the corner of her dim room, was the woman from the hills.

Isa took a step backward and bumped into the door-frame. Her heart sprinted inside her chest, and she felt the urge to scream rise up from her stomach, which was churning in terror.

The woman looked at her with a pained expression, seemingly as startled as Isa was. She held her hands at her side and watched silently.

Unsure what to do, Isa fumbled for the light switch. She flipped it up, casting a bright glow into the cold room. As she did, the ghost woman disappeared, leaving the corner as empty as it was when Isa'd woken up.

Almost instantly, the room seemed to warm up. She no longer felt the damp cold.

*What was she doing in here?* Isa thought, doing her best to control her breathing as a handful of questions sprung to life inside her brain. *Who is she? Did she follow me here?*

And more importantly, *what does she want?*

Isa paused, staring at the corner for a moment. Not sure she would like what might happen, she turned the light off again, half expecting the ghost to reappear. The corner was dimmed, but the ghost was still gone.

"Why were you here?" Isa asked the empty corner,

almost afraid she might get an answer. Nothing but silence followed.

She took a few brave steps toward the corner and spotted something on the ground. It looked like a worn bit of newspaper, yellowed with age. Isa crouched to pick it up and felt a lingering cold emanate from the thin paper.

Written on the scrap in a neat, flowing script were two words:

# CHAPTER 7
# INTO THE PAST

Isa stared at the piece of paper for a moment. She wondered if it was truly something the ghost had left behind or just a random scrap left on the floor of her aunt's house.

*Seventeen ladies?* Isa thought. *What could that possibly mean?*

Unsure of what to do with it, she put the piece of paper on her nightstand, underneath the coaster her glass of water sat on.

Still feeling a bit scared, Isa glanced over her shoulder to make sure the ghost woman hadn't materialized again. The corner was empty.

Even so, Isa wasn't sure she wanted to be in the house by herself. She had no idea if the woman might return or if something else equally creepy might happen. With that in mind, she grabbed her charging cord and returned to the kitchen. She plugged the cord into the center island's outlet and then into the bottom of her phone and waited for it to charge.

An icon lit up the screen, letting her know it was in the process of recharging. As she waited, she got lost in thought.

*Why am I not running out the front door?* Isa wondered. *I just saw the image of a dead woman in my bedroom!*

Isa didn't know if it was because she'd already seen the ghost outside too. Or maybe it was something different. Isa wondered if it was because she didn't think the ghost was dangerous or threatening.

Looking around again to see if she was being watched, Isa took a deep breath and spoke.

"Hey," she said. "I don't think you want to hurt me, and I don't want to disturb you."

Something in another room creaked, making her flinch.

"I'm not sure why you're here, though," Isa said. "Or who you are."

Just then, her phone vibrated slightly, making her jump. It was only an alert to let her know the phone was ready to be used while it charged.

Isa picked up her phone and unlocked it. She opened up a web browser and stared at the search window, wondering what exactly to look for.

She typed "HOLLYWOOD HILLS," then tapped SEARCH.

Somewhere around 154 million results were found within seconds. Most of them were pictures of the sign, the history of the sign, and odd questions people asked related to Hollywood and the Hollywood Hills.

*Guess I need to be more specific*, Isa thought.

Isa cleared the search and typed in a different set of words: "HOLLYWOOD HILLS GHOST."

Several articles and websites popped up. Some of them were movies about ghosts around Hollywood. Others were stories about reported haunted houses in the Hollywood area. Isa scrolled through the list, not really seeing anything that caught her eye.

"This isn't going to work," Isa mumbled.

*Am I the only one who knows about this ghost lady?*

Isa thought maybe there was some sort of clue buried somewhere on the internet but felt nervous keeping her focus on the screen. What if the ghost lady surprised her again?

Feeling a familiar chill, Isa looked up from her phone and across the room. Reflected in the glass on one of the doors of her aunt's hutch, she saw the woman's face, watching her.

Isa gasped.

She looked to see where the ghost might be standing but couldn't see anything. She looked back to the reflection and saw the woman's mouth was moving. It almost looked like she was pleading with Isa.

But no sound came out.

"I can't hear you," Isa whispered, feeling an iciness pass over her. "I . . . I don't know what you're saying."

Though she didn't feel like she was in danger, Isa couldn't help her heart from beating fast once again. It was like the rest of her body knew to be scared, even if she wasn't as much anymore.

"Are you trying to tell me something?" Isa asked.

The woman in the glass blinked and nodded once.

*She can hear me*, Isa thought and felt her ears ringing slightly as if this discovery were too much for her mind to take.

"How can I find out who you are?" Isa asked. "I want to know your name."

The woman mouthed something else, but just as before, nothing but silence emerged from her faded face.

"If you could just give me a hint," Isa said. "A sign or . . ."

*Sign.*

Isa looked down at her phone, then moved the cursor to the end of the search parameters and typed in an additional word: "SIGN."

"Hollywood Hills ghost sign," Isa read aloud.

The internet pulled up a number of new articles. At the top of the list was a story that immediately caught Isa's eye and interest: "The Haunted Hollywood Sign."

"Oh!" Isa gasped.

She opened the article. There was a photo of the Hollywood sign as it looked back in the old days: HOLLYWOODLAND.

Isa read the story beneath the image. It talked about a young actress named Margaret Whistler who wanted nothing more than to become a movie star. Margaret had taken roles in the theater and was pretty well-known. After finding success in New York, she had moved to California to chase her dreams. But it had been tough for her to break into the motion-picture business. She had been stuck doing plays. Then, one day, Margaret caught a lucky break. A production company signed her on as an actress to appear in one of their films.

Isa scrolled down to reveal another photo and sucked in her breath. A pretty young woman from the 1930s stared back at her. She had flawless skin and bright-green eyes. Isa immediately recognized her.

It was the ghost woman.

Isa looked up at the glass in the hutch's door and saw the same face looking back at her.

"Are you . . . Margaret?" Isa asked.

The woman's expression looked surprised, and she nodded slowly.

Isa could feel the surprise spread on her own face. She was pretty sure her mouth would dry out if she didn't close it.

"What happened to you?" Isa asked.

The woman stared back at her as if watching to see what she'd do next.

*Read the article,* Isa said to herself.

She looked down at her phone again and continued. The article explained that Margaret was given a chance to play a small part in a movie. One part of the film had her standing atop the letter H of the Hollywood sign, singing a song out into the world, proclaiming her love of the city below.

Isa put down the phone for a second and thought back to earlier in the day when she'd seen Margaret's ghost standing at the edge of the H. It had looked like she was singing.

*Was I seeing the scene from the movie?* Isa wondered.

*Is that why her ghost was lingering around the sign? Because they filmed her there?*

Isa read on, and almost immediately, her heart sank.

Tragedy struck, soon after Margaret's pivotal scene had been shot. The actress took a bad step as she turned to climb down the service ladder on the back of the letter. Before anyone could grab her, she fell fifty feet off of the letter H to her death.

The production crew and castmates rushed to try and help her, but it was too late. Margaret Whistler was dead. Her bright career as a movie star was over almost as soon as it began.

Isa set the phone down. She swallowed hard and felt like there were tears forming in her eyes.

"I'm so sorry," Isa whispered. "I'm sorry that happened to you, Margaret."

She glanced at the glass and saw the woman's face. Margaret glanced to her right, in the direction of the sign outside.

*Her spirit is somehow stuck there*, Isa thought. *And when I saw her, it looked like she was singing. I wonder if she keeps reliving her death? How horrible!*

As Isa reached for her phone, she heard the front door open.

"Sleeping beauty!" Aunt Violeta cried. "At last she's awake!"

"Whoa," Marta said, catching a glimpse at Isa's face. "What's wrong?"

Isa didn't realize that the tears had made a break for it down her cheeks. She was crying and quickly wiped them away with the back of her hand.

"Are you okay, Isabella?" Aunt Violeta said.

She rushed over to the kitchen's center island, set the takeout bags down, and put an arm around her niece. Isa lay her head against her aunt's shoulder.

"I'm okay," Isa said. "I just . . ."

"Did you get scared or something?" Aunt Violeta said. "I didn't mean for us to be gone so long. Traffic was awful and—"

"No, no," Isa said. "I saw the ghost again and—"

"You did?!" Marta cried. "Did you go back up in the hills? Why would you do that?"

"No," Isa said, frustrated that her sister was always interrupting her. "She's here, in the house. And you were right, Aunt Violeta. She doesn't want to hurt any of us."

Both Aunt Violeta and Marta were quiet. They both looked around as if trying to find the ghost.

"She's there," Isa said, pointing toward the large

hutch. But when she turned to see Margaret's face, the woman was gone.

"I don't see her," Marta said.

"She's gone now," Isa said. "You might've scared her off."

"That's a new one," Aunt Violeta said. "A ghost scared of the living."

Isa exhaled in an attempt to clear the sadness she'd taken on while reading Margaret's story. She explained to her aunt and sister how she'd woken up and found Margaret in the room, and how Isa'd been able to communicate with her.

"But you couldn't hear her," Marta said. "That's so creepy."

"That's what's so strange," Isa said. "It wasn't scary at all."

"It must not have been," Aunt Violeta said. "You didn't call and tell us to rush home."

"So why were you crying?" Marta asked. "Did you really miss us that much?"

Isa smiled. She knew her sister was just trying to cheer her up.

"No," Isa said. "I figured out who she was. I read a story about her online."

Isa recounted how Margaret Whistler had tried to get work in Hollywood, and when she finally appeared in a movie, she fell to her death while filming.

"It just hit me," Isa said. "It's so sad."

Both Aunt Violeta and Marta sat down at the counter as if the sad tale was hard to take standing up. None of them made any move to open the containers of Indian food they'd picked up in town.

"Can I see the article?" Marta asked.

Isa handed her phone to her sister, who scrolled through the article.

"Wow," Marta said. "Is that her?"

She held up the picture of Margaret smiling in a green dress. Her blond hair was pinned up on the sides, and her eyebrows were thin above her bright eyes. The photo had a real old-timey look to it.

"Yeah," Isa said. "I think so."

"That looks like an old black-and-white photo they colorized," Aunt Violeta said. "They didn't have color photos back then."

Marta read some more of the article, shaking her head. Her mouth was crimped into a sad frown as she read Margaret's story for herself.

" *'Seventeen Ladies,'* " Marta said, seemingly out of nowhere.

Immediately, Isa perked up.

"What did you say?" Isa asked quickly.

"It talks about the name of the movie she was in when she died," Marta said. "*Seventeen Ladies.*"

# CHAPTER 8
# NIGHT WHISPERS

Isa had that strange sensation pass through her again. It was like when she was working on a tough problem in her math homework and the solution suddenly made sense.

"Her movie," Isa said. "That's what the note meant!"

Both her sister and her aunt seemed surprised by Isa's outburst.

"Note?" Marta asked. "The ghost lady is leaving you notes?"

"Her name is Margaret," Isa reminded her. "And yeah, I think so. When I saw her in my room after my nap, there was an old piece of newspaper left behind with the words *Seventeen Ladies* on it."

"And you think she left it for you to find, Isabella?" Aunt Violeta asked.

Isa nodded.

Marta looked doubtful and glanced at their aunt as if to see if she was believing such a thing was possible.

"I don't know," Marta said. "I'm having a hard time—"

"I'll go get it," Isa said.

She dashed to her room, found the yellowed piece of paper, and brought it back out to the kitchen. She handed it to her sister and aunt.

"Okay," Marta admitted, shaking her head slowly. "That's weird."

Aunt Violeta studied it closely.

"But what does it mean?" Isa seemed to ask herself out loud—or maybe even the paper itself. "What's she trying to say?"

Marta shrugged. "Maybe she wanted to advertise the one movie she was in," she suggested. "That's some serious promotion, hanging around after you're dead to let people know about it."

There was a loud knock from the other side of the room, making all three of them jump.

"I don't think Margaret liked that," Isa said, glancing in the direction of the sound. Despite looking, she couldn't see the ghost.

"Sorry, sorry," Marta said, making an exaggerated cringe face.

Aunt Violeta finally put down the scrap of paper and touched her upper lip with her finger.

"I'll admit, I've never heard of this movie she was in," she said. "When was it filmed?"

Isa took the phone back from Marta and scrolled through the article, searching for dates. She finally landed on the date of Margaret's death.

"1932 was when she had her accident," Isa said, choosing her words carefully.

"Then they probably finished filming and putting the movie together shortly after," Aunt Violeta said.

"You think they still made the movie even after one of their stars . . . you know," Marta said, seemingly avoiding the words that might trigger an upset response from Margaret.

Aunt Violeta nodded. "Sad as her story was, movies cost a lot to make, and it's highly likely they finished the movie without her."

"I wonder if all of her parts were filmed before that happened," Isa said, then realized she could find out all of those answers fairly quickly.

She opened a new search window and typed in the words "SEVENTEEN LADIES MOVIE."

Instantly, it displayed information about the old black-and-white movie. There were even webpages and articles that talked about Margaret Whistler's untimely death and how the hills were haunted by her ghost.

"They finished it all right," Isa said, looking at other pictures of Margaret embedded into the story.

"There's a saying in the entertainment business," Aunt Violeta said, her voice taking on a somber tone. "The show must go on."

"The weird thing is," Isa said, pausing for a moment, "I think Margaret was trying to tell me something."

Marta shook her head back and forth quickly.

"Okay, that's pretty much the most terrifying thing I've ever heard," she said. "Can we please stop talking about this?"

"But she's here," Isa said. "It's pretty obvious something is tying her to this place."

"Well," Marta was quick to reply, "according to the article, she was tied to the hills. Now, somehow, she's tied to *you*."

Hearing that out loud made Isa pause for a moment in fear.

*Did I draw Margaret to me when I went up into the hills?* Isa wondered. *What if Margaret follows me around wherever I go? Will she follow me back home to Iowa?*

"I don't know what to do," Isa admitted. "I have no idea why she's stuck here or anything."

"Maybe her soul is lost because she met an unfortunate end," Aunt Violeta suggested. "And she's stuck here, unable to pass on to the next place."

"Do you really think so?" Isa asked. She thought it was bad enough that Margaret had died just as her career was finally taking off, but then to be stuck near the place where she had passed away? It sounded too tragic for words.

"Is that how people become ghosts?" Marta asked. "You have an accident, and then you . . . er, something horrible happens? That's it? You're stuck here forever?"

Aunt Violeta shrugged and reached for the bags of food. She pulled a few of the containers from the takeout bags and set them out.

"I'm not sure anyone knows for sure, Martalina," Aunt Violeta replied. "There are people who don't even believe in ghosts. I can honestly say I'm no longer one of them, girls."

Isa nodded. She hadn't really considered lost spirits or ghosts at all before coming to her aunt's house. Now, it seemed it was all she could think about.

"So if something happens to you, you're stuck there?" Isa asked.

*If that's the case, there have to be ghosts everywhere,* she thought. *Is there something more to it than that?*

"I don't have the answers, Isabella," Aunt Violeta said with a light sigh, and she opened up the food, releasing the steam from the containers.

"If so, I'm going to be extra careful," Marta said.

"I'll even wear my helmet that messes up my hair next time I ride my bike."

The three of them laughed and decided it was time to eat.

———

Later that night, when the house was silent and Isa was in her bed, she stared up at the ceiling. Though she was tired and it was late in the evening, she was finding it hard to sleep. It wasn't that she was scared of Margaret, but thinking about her spirit being stuck kept rattling around in Isa's brain.

*Is she stuck here forever? Will she follow me wherever I go?*

She didn't know how or what kept ghosts locked into the world of the living, but she wished there were something she could do to put Margaret's soul at ease.

"What can I do?" Isa whispered.

She half expected the room to grow cold, which seemed to be an indication that Margaret's ghost was close by. But the air around her remained the same temperature.

*I wish I knew what she was trying to tell me,* Isa thought. She'd heard about paranormal television shows where people went into haunted places with the sole purpose of communicating with the dead.

Since she wasn't going to fall asleep anytime soon, she grabbed her phone to do some research. After finding a couple of websites devoted to the paranormal programs, Isa learned about EVPs, which she found stood for "electronic voice phenomenon." EVPs were voices that some investigators captured, supposedly from ghosts.

Isa watched a video of a group of people sitting around in the dark, using recorders and asking questions. After they were done, they played the recordings back, listening for answers. She could feel her heart rate increase as creepy, whispering voices would occasionally come through.

"Okay," Isa whispered, stopping the video. "That's enough."

She took a moment to calm down. The voices she had heard in the online videos sounded angry. One of them had told the investigators to "get out." At least, it *sounded* like that's what it had said.

Isa flipped through her phone's built-in apps and found the voice recorder. It was simple enough to use:

Touch the button to record, and the phone's microphone would pick up any noise.

*But will it pick up Margaret's?*

Unsure if it was a great idea or not, Isa decided to try it. The moment it got spooky, she would turn it off.

She touched the red button on her screen and saw the time start, showing that it was recording. A little bar ran across the middle of the screen. When Isa shifted in the bed a little, she could see the waveforms move, showing it had picked up the sound.

"Okay," Isa whispered into the room. "Guess I'll give this a try."

She sat up and looked around the room, thinking she'd see Margaret's face. The woman was nowhere to be found, making Isa wonder if Margaret had given up on her and had gone back to stand on the H again.

"Margaret, are you here?"

Her voice sounded small in the empty, quiet room. She looked at the waveform to see if it moved at all. It was straight as it cut across the middle of her phone. Nothing was picked up.

Isa tried to think of the things the pros in the paranormal videos had asked. They had all sounded confident and brave. She wasn't really scared, just unsure of what she was doing.

"If you're here, can you talk to me?"

Isa watched the screen again. Still nothing.

Then the air began to cool almost instantly.

"You're here, aren't you?" Isa whispered, shivering slightly.

There was a hitch on the waveform.

"Will you try and talk to me?" Isa asked. "If I can, I want to know what you're trying to tell me."

Isa wrapped her covers around her a little more, trying to stay as warm as she could. She knew Margaret didn't mean her any harm, but it was still a little creepy, knowing that the spirit of someone who'd died decades ago was in the room with her.

"You were trying to tell me something," Isa said, "earlier in the evening, but I couldn't hear you."

She exhaled and could see her breath. Margaret was in the room with her. Isa took a deep breath, waiting to see if the young movie star's form would appear.

"Can you tell me what you were saying?" Isa asked. She found herself looking up at the ceiling as if to keep herself from jumping if the ghost materialized before her.

She glanced down for a moment and saw that the recorder had captured something she couldn't hear with her own ears. Isa knew she shouldn't be too excited. It seemed to move with any sort of sound she made, including her breathing and the chattering of her teeth.

Isa pushed the red button to end the EVP session. The app told her that NEW RECORDING 1 was 2:19 long.

Isa pushed the button and could hear her own voice. There was no answer when she asked, "*Margaret, are you here?*"

She kept listening. There was no answer to her next question either.

When she asked, "*You're here, aren't you?*" there was an answer.

"*Yes.*"

Isa dropped her phone harmlessly into the blankets covering her lap. She stared at the phone and then looked up, again certain she'd see Margaret. But she didn't.

The recording kept playing, and Isa sat and listened to it.

When she asked Margaret what she had been saying earlier in the evening, there was a fractured, airy reply.

It sounded as if the woman were sad and whispering her response.

The only words Isa could make out were "never" and "film."

Isa let the recording play out, staring at the phone, almost in shock. As she did, she felt the room start to warm up again.

Margaret was gone.

# CHAPTER 9

# LAST REQUEST

Isa sat in her bed for a few minutes as the gravity of what she'd just done washed over her. She'd captured a voice from a ghost. She'd actually talked to and gotten a response from someone who had lived and died a long time ago.

It was a little bit overwhelming.

*But what was the ghost saying?*

" *'Never'* . . . *'film,'* " Isa whispered to herself, running the words around in her brain a bit. It sounded airy and distant, as if Margaret had been trying to whisper to her from across a room. Instead, it was from the beyond or wherever it was that ghosts existed.

"You never wanted to be in film?" Isa asked, trying to put the pieces together.

She realized that couldn't be right. The articles she'd read about Margaret had said that being in movies was exactly what Margaret had wanted. And she had been in movies until she had met her unfortunate end.

Isa thought about it some more but was unable to

decipher what the words meant. She almost wanted to try and ask Margaret more questions but wasn't sure it was possible. She had read that paranormal experts believe it takes an incredible amount of energy for ghosts to do anything.

Asking them to talk, make noise, or move objects could sap their energy.

Isa wondered if that's why Margaret was gone—she just didn't have any energy to do much more.

Isa played the clip again, turning the volume up as high as it would go. The tiny speakers at the bottom of her phone hissed in the pauses between Isa's questions. When Margaret's voice did come through, it sounded almost distorted, as if the volume were too loud.

"That's not going to work," Isa said. She lowered the volume and played it again. She listened closely to the recording again, paying close attention to the gaps between the words she could hear Margaret saying.

But there was something else, just faint enough for it to be tough to hear through the phone's speakers.

*Maybe my earbuds will help me hear better.* Isa slipped out of bed. She tiptoed to her carry-on backpack, unzipped the front pocket, and fished out a pair of earbuds. As she headed back to her phone and bed, she popped them into her ears and plugged them into her phone.

Once she'd climbed back into bed, she pressed play.

The audio was too loud and made her wince as she jammed the button to lower the volume. She waited until the light ringing in her ears subsided before starting the EVP recording again.

She listened to the entire thing, bracing herself for the part where she got to the end where Margaret said, "*never . . . film.*"

As the part played, she heard whispers before and after the gaps between the words. They were just quiet enough that she could barely hear them. Isa skipped the recording back a few seconds and started it again.

She turned up the volume. As Margaret spoke, Isa pressed the earbuds as far into her ears as she could.

"*I never got to see my film,*" the light, sad voice in her ear whispered.

Isa almost cried out loud in triumph but slapped a hand over her mouth to stop herself. As soon as she regained her composure, the reality of what it all meant was horribly sad to her.

*Margaret Whistler never got to see the one and only*

*film she'd been in,* Isa thought. *She died before* Seventeen Ladies *was completed.*

Isa thought about everything that must've happened after the accident in Hollywood Hills. She wondered how Margaret's family had handled the news. She thought about the other actors who might've been in the scene with Margaret. She imagined the horror of anyone who had been anywhere near the tragedy.

*Did Margaret have other scenes to film? Did they change the movie because of what happened?* Isa couldn't stop her mind from thinking about everything surrounding Margaret's death.

More than anything, she felt sadness over what had happened to Margaret Whistler and was crushed she'd never gotten to see her film.

*Is that what's keeping her here?*

———

Isa could hardly sleep. When she woke up after a few hours, she waited impatiently for both Marta and her aunt to wake up. She considered being extra noisy to rouse her sister but decided that wasn't the best idea.

While she waited, she decided to look for *Seventeen Ladies.* Sitting in the kitchen with her phone plugged in, she searched the internet for places where she could watch the old film. None of the usual video-sharing sites seemed to have it—or, at least, not the entire movie.

Isa found a link that said "SEVENTEEN LADIES" and clicked on it. It showed a two-minute clip of the old black-and-white film. In it, a man with dark, slick hair and a fantastic mustache was eating dinner with a woman in a white dress wearing a sparkly headband. Her hair was long and blond.

"Is that her?" Isa whispered to herself. She watched the scene, and when the woman turned her head, she could see it wasn't Margaret. The woman on the video had a longer, more sharply shaped nose. Her eyes were darker too.

The room stayed the same temperature, letting Isa know that Margaret wasn't there with her anyway.

*This isn't going to do it*, Isa realized. *She needs to see the whole thing.*

Isa wasn't sure that letting the ghost watch her film would be all that it took to free her. She wasn't even sure such a thing were possible. She just knew that if she could find the movie and let her see it, Margaret might find some peace, even if it were only temporary.

Isa spent the next twenty minutes looking for other websites that might have the movie. One of them boasted having a link to the *entire* film, but when she clicked on it, an error screen came up, letting her know the webpage was gone.

Thinking it might be something they could buy, Isa went to online shopping sites. She typed in "SEVENTEEN LADIES" there and found nothing besides an old movie poster for the film that cost around seven hundred dollars.

"Nope," Isa said. "Not helpful."

When her aunt finally shuffled into the kitchen and headed right for the coffee maker, Isa sprang up and told her everything—how she had captured Margaret's voice, how she had figured out what Margaret was saying.

"She never got to see her movie!" Isa exclaimed as the coffee started to brew. "We have to change that."

Aunt Violeta nodded and appeared to struggle to reach the same energy level as her niece.

"So you want to show a ghost the movie she was in?"

"Well, yeah," Isa said. "Does that sound ridiculous?"

Aunt Violeta poured herself a cup and set the pot back on the burner.

"Ridiculous?" she asked. "I think it's the sweetest idea I've ever heard."

The two of them set out to search for the movie in any way, shape, or form they could find it. Aunt Violeta even worked from her laptop across from Isa at the kitchen's center island. They both called out to each other any time they had a lead on where they might be able to find it.

Isa made a heartbreaking realization.

"The movie is so old, it was never even put on DVD or Blu-ray," she said.

"I think that speaks to the film's popularity," Aunt Violeta said. "If no one is looking for it, they're not going to release it that way."

"I want to see it!" Isa cried. "And Margaret does too. Doesn't that count for something?"

Aunt Violeta laughed, and they got back to searching.

"What's VHS?" Isa asked a few minutes later.

"Did you find it?" Aunt Violeta asked.

"I'm not sure," Isa admitted. "But there's a store in Hollywood that claims to have all kinds of old movies, many of them on VHS."

Aunt Violeta smiled. "They're like tapes with movies on them," she said.

"Tapes?" Isa asked.

"It's how we watched movies before DVDs," Aunt Violeta explained. "Big, clunky things."

Isa walked over and showed her aunt what she'd found. It was an online review of a place on Sunset Boulevard called Gold Star Video. The reviewer said it was like taking a step back in time, and the store boasted the biggest collection of golden-era films on the West Coast.

"Can we call them?" Aunt Violeta asked. "See if they have it?"

Isa shrugged and searched the review for a link to the store's website. There wasn't one.

"This place must be really old school," Isa said. "No website."

She typed the words "GOLD STAR VIDEO" into the search bar. A listing came up with the store's phone number.

Isa entered the number and switched the call to speakerphone. After what seemed like twenty rings, a scratchy recording came on. A man, who sounded like he was close to one hundred years old, spoke.

"Thank you for calling Gold Star Video, where the stars are always shining," the old guy said. "If you are hearing my voice, that means we're closed. Our normal store hours are 9 a.m. to 7 p.m., or whenever I feel like closing. We are not open on Sundays, so you'll probably need to find something else to do. Thank you."

Isa and Aunt Violeta looked at each other.

"Wow," they both said.

Isa looked at the clock on her phone. Gold Star Video was due to open in less than one hour.

"What do you think?" Isa said. "Should we go find a VSH of that movie?"

"VHS," Aunt Violeta corrected, smiling. "And yes."

"I'll go get Marta," Isa said.

———

After driving for nearly an hour, they pulled in front of a small, almost hidden shop nestled between a comedy club and a weatherworn theater. The store's yellow sign with red letters was cracked in places, and the front window was plastered with movie posters that had been almost completely bleached out by the sun.

"So this is what we've been looking for?" Marta said from the back seat. "This place looks like anything but a gold star."

Isa and Aunt Violeta had caught her sister up on the way to Gold Star Video, but now Isa was beginning to wonder if the trip was going to be worth it. The place looked almost abandoned.

"Are they even open?" Isa asked.

"Let's find out," Aunt Violeta suggested, putting her car into park.

The three of them climbed out and approached

the old store. There was a sign on the door displaying the store hours, the lettering looking like it had been written in blue crayon.

Marta walked up to the window and looked at the old posters, a disapproving scowl on her face.

"Yeah," she said. "Pretty sure this place is closed."

Isa ignored her sister and went to the front door and pulled. The door didn't open.

"Shoot," Isa said, turning to her family. "I guess they're—"

Before she could even finish, the bolt to the door clicked, and the door opened part way.

"Can I help you?" a voice said through the crack in the door.

"Um, yeah," Isa said, glancing at her aunt for a moment. "We're looking for a movie and wanted to see if—"

"Well," the voice said, more enthusiastically than before. "Come on in, and let's get you situated!" The door creaked open.

The three of them looked at each other, and Aunt Violeta shrugged.

"C'mon," Marta said. "I gotta see what this place looks like inside!"

# CHAPTER 10

# END CREDITS

Isa, Marta, and Aunt Violeta stepped through the doorway and into a place that made all of their jaws drop. Everywhere they looked, there were stacks and stacks of rectangular boxes. They looked like books but didn't seem to have pages.

"VHS tapes," Aunt Violeta whispered to her nieces. "Those are movies. Old ones."

The man who had opened the door for them had already made his way to a cluttered counter. He was hunched over the counter where there were at least twenty more movies scattered. One of them looked like it was opened up, the thing's brown tape spooling out onto the glass.

The old guy adjusted his thick glasses and smiled, showing off a set of light-yellow teeth. He wore a nametag pinned to his short-sleeve shirt that simply said "Norman."

"Welcome to Gold Star," Norman said. "Which film were you looking for?"

Isa had to stop staring at all of the videos stacked nearly to the ceiling, overstuffing the shelves and scattered around on the floor.

"Hi," Isa said. "We're looking for *Seventeen Ladies*."

"Well, you only found one old fella," Norman said, then laughed like he'd been waiting decades to try out that joke.

Marta actually laughed too.

"I like this guy," she whispered.

"That's pretty funny," Isa said, being polite. "But it's a movie from the 1930s and has an actress named Margaret Whistler in it."

Isa braced herself for a joke about whistling, but one never came.

"Hmm," Norman said. "I don't recognize that title, but these days I tend to forget more than I remember."

He walked along the back of his counter to a wall of VHS tapes. None of them seemed to be in any sort of order.

"It wasn't very popular, I'm afraid," Aunt Violeta said, glancing around the store with her eyebrows raised.

"Yes, yes," Norman said. "Marge Whistlehouse, you say?"

"Well," Isa replied, not sure if Norman was just trying to be funny. "Margaret Whistler. It was her one and only film, sadly."

Norman grunted something as he rifled through a stack perched at the end of the counter. Some of them teetered and started to fall. Isa rushed forward and caught them before they hit the ground.

"Thanks for the grab, little lady," Norman said, pushing his glasses back up onto his bulbous nose.

Marta walked around the store, gazing up at the seemingly endless piles of tapes.

"How do you ever find anything in here?" Marta asked, making Isa immediately blush in embarrassment.

"A little patience and a good eye," Norman said. "Sadly, I'm short on both."

"Then we'll help you," Marta said.

As they helped Norman search, Isa marveled at how many movies there were, almost all of them black-and-white films with movie stars she'd never heard of.

Isa saw one with a man and a woman staring up into the night sky called *Grab the Moon*. She got excited when she saw the word *Dies*, partially obscured at the bottom of a crooked stack of tapes.

*Could it be* Seventeen Ladies? she wondered.

When she crouched down, she saw the full title: *At Dawn the Night Dies*.

"We're never going to find this thing," Marta said. "You know that, right?"

"Shh," Isa hissed.

"Are you sure you want that movie?" Norman said. "Couldn't interest you in a Herbert Willowby classic like *The Sloppiest Sir*?"

"No thank you," Isa said. "We really only want to see that one."

"Okay," Norman said. "Then I guess you're all set."

"What?!" Marta cried.

All three of them headed back toward the counter

where Norman was standing, smiling proudly, a worn copy of *Seventeen Ladies* in his hand.

"Is that it?" Isa asked, looking at the box.

Norman nodded and handed it to her. "She's not listed in the credits, but that's the one. Shot in 1932 right here in Hollywood."

A chill went down Isa's spine hearing Norman say that. She wondered if he knew just how accurate his words were.

Isa studied the box for a moment. It had a bunch of young women on the cover and a man with fancy hair wearing a tuxedo standing in front of them. He had his hands out and his eyebrows raised as if to say, "Can you believe this?"

"Wow, thank you for finding it," Isa said. "How much do we owe you?"

Norman waved her off and smiled. "Nothing," he said. "I don't get many customers anymore, just friends with a true love of the cinema. Bring it back when you're done, and we'll find you something else to watch."

The three of them thanked Norman again for his help, and he escorted them to the door, urging them to come back and see him again soon. As soon as they stepped out into the bright sunlight, the door behind them was closed and bolted.

*Yes,* Isa thought again. *It's like a different world out here.*

———————

As soon as they got back to the house, their aunt disappeared into the back spare bedroom. It was, they'd learned when they had gotten the full tour, what she called her "junk" room. It was where she put all the stuff she hadn't sorted out yet.

"What is she doing?" Marta asked.

Isa shrugged and held the movie tight. She was almost afraid to drop it, considering it might be the last copy of the old movie in existence. Or, at least, nearby.

A moment later, there was a sound of stuff crashing down, followed by the sound of their aunt cursing in Spanish.

"You girls didn't hear that!" she called from the back room.

"Are you okay?" Isa asked. "Can we help?"

There was no answer, and as Isa made a move to see if her aunt was still alive, Aunt Violeta emerged from the hallway with a large silver box in her arms. A twisted black power cord dangled from the back end.

"What is that?" Marta asked.

Aunt Violeta walked past them and headed to the television mounted above a floating shelf. She set the box down and untangled the cord.

"This, girls," their aunt announced, "is a VCR."

*VHS, VCR*, Isa thought. *Who can keep it straight?*

Isa looked closely at the box and saw a thin, rectangular door on the front of the device. She figured it out.

"That thing will play the movie, right?"

Aunt Violeta nodded. "Let's hope so," she said. "I haven't used it in ages."

She stood there for a moment as if running through a checklist of what they needed to get the machine running. Her pointer finger popped up, and she went back into the hallway.

"Let's hope she comes back out in one piece," Marta said.

Their aunt returned with a cord that had a red, a white, and a yellow plug on each end. She plugged one set into the back of the VCR and the other set into the side of her TV. A moment later, she plugged the power cord into the wall.

"That's it," Aunt Violeta announced. "I think it's showtime!"

As Marta and her aunt tried to figure out what chan-
nel or input to switch the TV to, Isa glanced around.
She didn't see Margaret anywhere and couldn't feel the
telltale cold of her presence.

"Margaret," Isa whispered. "We're going to play your
movie. Please come and watch it with us."

Isa knew she wouldn't be able to hear the starlet's
ghost but wondered if Margaret had heard her.

She turned to see Marta watch in fascination as Aunt
Violeta slipped the video out of the sleeve and insert
it into the VCR. The machine made a weird whirring
noise as it swallowed the tape up.

"So weird," Marta said, as if watching some ancient
ritual.

Isa tried to feel if the air had changed in the room.
It didn't seem any colder than it had been a few moments ago. She looked around again, hoping to see the
ghost woman's face in her aunt's hutch, standing in the
corner, anywhere.

Margaret was nowhere to be found.

The screen displayed large blue letters that said
"Play" above a scratchy black background. A fuzzy line
appeared at the bottom of the TV. As if on autopilot,

Aunt Violeta walked over to the VCR and fiddled with something.

"Tracking," Aunt Violeta said. "One of the big drawbacks of VHS tapes."

They watched the video display a warning about the FBI cracking down on people who copy video recordings, letting viewers know it was considered theft.

"Who'd want to steal these movies?" Marta whispered.

"Shh," Isa warned. "What if—"

"The ghost lady hears?"

"Just be quiet," Isa said.

As she said that, she felt the room begin to chill.

"Aunt Violeta," Marta said, "can you turn the AC off?"

Isa smiled and watched the goose bumps rise along her arms. The tiny light hairs stood straight up as the living room got chillier.

"She's here," Isa whispered.

"Perfect," Marta replied, sinking into the couch as if to hide.

They watched the movie, which turned out to be the story of a widowed man with seventeen daughters or, as the title suggested, *Seventeen Ladies*. Each of the daughters were slowly introduced in the movie, and each of them had a different hope or dream they wanted to achieve. It was up to their hapless dad to try and keep them from getting into trouble.

Aunt Violeta smiled. "It was a different world back then," she said. "There was a time when people believed women couldn't do anything without a man's help."

"That's ridiculous," Isa said.

"Where's your friend, Isa?" Marta asked. "I haven't seen her yet."

"I'm not sure," Isa replied. She almost wondered if they'd somehow gotten the wrong video. Margaret hadn't shown up on screen yet.

A horrible thought crossed her mind: *Had they cut her part from the film? Because of her death?* She didn't think so, as the websites she had found about Margaret spoke of *Seventeen Ladies* being her first and final film.

They continued to watch as one of the daughters wanted to join the circus and become a lion tamer. The poor leading man who played their dad ended up nearly getting mauled to death by a fake lion that Isa guessed was supposed to be funny.

The cold got colder the longer they watched the movie.

And then . . . she appeared.

All three of the Rodriguez ladies cheered when Margaret Whistler came onto the screen. She played Gloria Preston, the youngest daughter of Walter, the widowed father of the seventeen ladies.

When Margaret spoke on-screen as Gloria, she sounded sophisticated and well-rehearsed, like all old-timey movie actors seemed to. They all watched in fascination as Margaret told her father her dream of singing before the entire city.

And in the movie, the scene changed to a dream sequence. There, as Isa had seen just yesterday, Margaret Whistler was standing on top of the H of the HOLLYWOODLAND sign, singing her heart out to anyone in the valley below who happened to be listening.

The mood in the room went from elation to sadness as they realized what happened moments after the scene was shot. They were witnessing the last few moments of a young Hollywood dreamer's life.

And just like that, the scene shifted to another one of the Preston daughters. The shift in story was abrupt, and Isa knew it had to be because Margaret had passed on. But, as Aunt Violeta had said, "The show must go on."

"She was great," Isa said, more to herself than anyone else. Both her sister and aunt nodded.

"Yeah," Marta said. "Probably the best of the sisters for sure."

"A really talented young lady," Aunt Violeta agreed. "Taken away from the world far too soon."

The movie ended a few moments later, and Isa felt a tear trickle down her cheek.

"I know it was supposed to be a comedy," Marta said, wiping her own eyes. "But that was really kind of sad."

Isa nodded. "I just hope Margaret got to see it," she said. "And could see how well she did."

Just then, Isa felt something cold press down on her shoulder. From her seat on the couch, she felt as if she were standing with her back to an open freezer door. The smell of something flowery followed.

"Do you guys smell that?" Marta asked. "It smells like—"

"Lavender perfume," Aunt Violeta said.

"She's standing right behind me," Isa whispered. "And she's got her hand on my shoulder."

The movie credits played until the screen was hissing with static, their cue to stop the tape and to "Be kind and rewind."

"I hope this brought you some sort of peace,

Margaret," Isa said, touching her shoulder as if meaning to place her hand on top of the ghost's.

As the coldness left the room and her shoulder lightened, they could all hear a faint whisper in the TV's static: *"It did . . ."*

# AUTHOR'S NOTE

I don't think it was possible to set a Haunted States of America book in California and *not* have it tied in somehow with Hollywood and movies. As a huge film nerd, I actually lived there for a short time to try and break into filmmaking. I loved the weather, palm trees, ocean, and how strange of a place it can be at times. I wanted to make sure Isabella Rodriquez got to experience it that way too.

I used the story of real-life actress Peg Entwistle as a jumping-off point for *A Starlet's Shadow*. Peg, like Margaret Whistler, was a young actress who wanted to break into film. Both of them were in only one movie before their death in Hollywood Hills.

The movie Peg was in was called *Thirteen Women*. I didn't know anything about the movie, but to keep it sort of close, I called Margaret's film *Seventeen Ladies*. I completely made up the plot about a widowed man who has seventeen daughters. Kind of a ridiculous premise, but I thought it fit in with the "old Hollywood" types of movies.

Another thing I changed was the cause of the ghost's death. In this story, Margaret died during a freak accident while filming a movie. In real life, Peg died by suicide. This was not a change that I took lightly but ultimately one that I felt was appropriate, given the book's depth and readership.

In the book, Isa had a little trouble getting up the hill to get close to the sign, but in real life, it's a lot more difficult. Because of littering and vandalism, the city has closed the paths that used to take tourists right up to the sign. But those who were able to get close really have reported smelling Peg's perfume and seeing her up near the Hollywood Hills sign; however, those reports say the scent is gardenias, not lavender.

What about other places in this story? The restaurant that Aunt Violeta took the girls to in the beginning is based on a place called Musso & Frank Grill. It really has been around since 1919 and is just as dark and classic-looking today. But to my knowledge, there isn't a Gold Star Video store in Hollywood, and there certainly isn't an old fellow named Norman working there. I liked the idea that this guy was running a store that held onto these old movies in a format that is all but extinct. Made it seem like Isa and her family were trying to find a needle in a haystack!

If you ever have the chance to go to the West Coast, there's plenty to do! Theme parks, oceans, museums, and tons of sightseeing. Try and get up into Hollywood to see the sign, even if it's from a distance. After all, Hollywood produces a lot of stories . . . including ghost stories.

# ABOUT THE AUTHOR

Thomas Kingsley Troupe has been making up stories ever since he was in short pants. As an "adult," he's the author of a whole lot of books for kids. When he's not writing, he enjoys movies, biking, taking naps, and investigating ghosts as a member of the Twin Cities Paranormal Society. Raised in "Nordeast" Minneapolis, he now lives in Woodbury, Minnesota, with his awe-inspiring family.

# ABOUT THE ILLUSTRATORS

Maggie Ivy is a freelance illustrator and artist who lives and works in the Ozark area in Arkansas. She found her love for art at an early age and pursued it with passion. She graduated from The Florence Academy of Art in 2010. She loves narrative elements and story-building moments, and seeks to implement them in her own work.

Clonefront Entertainment is a London-based art studio, focusing on illustrations for books and film. Szabolcs Pal, the illustrator for the interior of this series, is one of the fresh talents at Clonefront. He comes from the graphic novel industry, and worked on character developments for movies before moving into book illustration.

# DISCOVER MORE

HAUNTED STATES of AMERICA

## BY THOMAS KINGSLEY TROUPE

A CALIFORNIA
GHOST STORY

A COLORADO
GHOST STORY

A FLORIDA
GHOST STORY

A LOUISIANA
GHOST STORY

A MINNESOTA
GHOST STORY

A NEW JERSEY
GHOST STORY

A TENNESSEE
GHOST STORY

A TEXAS
GHOST STORY